HAIFA PUBLISHING COMPANY LTD.

Special thanks to
Tamara Frankel, George & Debbie Frankel,
Shelly & Ian Schorr, David Schorr,
Michael & Julie Seelig, and Rick Allred.

Manufactured in PRC
2 4 6 8 10 9 7 5 3 1
ISBN 9781732934009

HAIFA PUBLISHING COMPANY LTD.

FROM
NEIGH
TO ZEBRA

There once was a horse who was happy and gay,
confessing his love with each nicker and neigh.

"My zebra's angelic; she's brilliant, she's bold!
She shines even brighter than diamonds and gold!"

Miss Zebra was also in love with Sir Horse...

...but this type of love was *forbidden*, of course.

The horses brayed loudly - "NO ONE APPROVES!"
The zebras were *furious*, kicking their hooves.

They chanted these mantras. They groaned and they griped.
But *love* can be stronger than skin that is striped.

The horse was forlorn.

He was sad. He was blue.

He bowed down his head

in the hullabaloo.

He then racked his brain; he considered and thought...

He needed a plan; soon a plan's what he got!

A light bulb went off up on top of his head.

"I *know* what to do!" the horse finally said.

He went into town and he ordered a suit;
the finest of finest, with big stripes to boot.

He had the garb tailored to fit like a glove,
then smoothed it on tightly to be with his love.

Across town, the zebra, who loved with such force,

she painted her stripes to be one with her horse.

So when they next met, this heroine and hero,
a horse with some stripes; a zebra with zero,

well, no one could tell which was which, who was who,
but *still* they mismatched with the whole switcheroo!

The outrage raged on but they weathered the storm

and true to themselves, they rejected the norm.

The horse with his stripes and his love with her mane –

a beautiful pair – one striped and one plain.

No brute could diminish their *spark* or their *light*.

Though some kept protesting, their *bark* had less *bite*.

Years later I heard that they'd had a sweet child.

I saw an old picture and gasped as I smiled...

This strong, handsome boy – their strapping young lad
had fur that was rainbow on skin that was plaid!

Now here's where the story gets far, far too sappy...

With love, kids, and rainbows, they ended up happy.

**LOVED IT?
AWW... WE LOVE
YOU TOO!**

Wanna confess your love to everyone
you know, just like Sir Horse on page 1?

We would be forever in your debt if you were to be so kind as
to write a review on Amazon or share the book with your people.
We'll send you the squeeziest virtual bear hug!

We're so happy you found this book and that you're
helping us make the world a kinder place,
so here's a little somethin' somethin' for YOU.

Head to www.RainbowZebra.co/gift to collect a free surprise
just for being your awesome self.